A BOOK OF SHORTS

Short Stories and Poems

Julie Vellacott

CONTENTS

INTRODUCTION

'The time has come,' the walrus said, 'to talk of many things: of shoes and ships - and sealing wax - of cabbages and kings.'

Lewis Carroll said it for me.

Sorting through poorly filed stories, poems and random thoughts was a lot like going down a rabbithole. I've hauled some to the surface and put them together with no purpose or plan except that I rather like them. I hope you do too.

Some have previously appeared on my website or in collections, some are being aired for the first time.

Some are fiction, some are fact, some a mix. Gran is very real, you couldn't make her up.

Here is Lewis Carroll again, in *Through the Looking Glass*. Again.

"'When I use a word,' Humpty Dumpty said in rather a scornful tone, 'it means just what I choose it to mean — neither more nor less.'
'The question is,' said Alice, 'whether you can make words mean so many different things.'
'The question is,' said Humpty Dumpty, 'which is to be master — that's all.'"

AT GRAN'S PLACE

Where once I saw my mother in the mirror every morning, more and more I'm seeing my grandmother. That is my mother's mother – so it's not really surprising.

Only in the face though, and slightly in the hairstyle. Hair pulled back into a French pleat held in place with pins and combs; where she used a twist from the hairline to create height I rely on teasing and hairspray. Gran's dresses – grandmothers didn't wear trousers then – were always brown or blue with plentiful pleats and gathers to bulk out her small figure. She was a tiny woman but one for whom the adjective indomitable was created. She didn't smile a lot, she'd probably say she didn't have a lot to smile about. She was levelheaded, not overly sentimental. Not given to gushing over her offspring or even her offspring's offspring. Like many pragmatic people who don't show much emotion, when she smiled the sun came out.

Her husband, my grandfather, died the year before I was born. They had moved from the farm to the seaside suburb of Wynnum, to a house right on the railway line. Gran grew pumpkins and melons on the steep bank that ran from the back fence to the railway tracks. Our hearts were in our mouths as we watched her scrambling around weeding and watering and picking the produce. Every day we expected to hear she'd slid down into the path of a train. But of course that didn't happen. She had responsibilities and was as careful in the garden as she was with life in general.

We kids used to stay with her during the summer holidays. It was a break for our parents left at home and we enjoyed the independence Gran allowed us. We took off to the tidal pool most days, togs under our shorts or playsuits, rolled up towel held firmly under an arm. No lifesavers come to mind when I picture that rough concrete pool, but vivid images remain of the grazes sustained while using the not-very-slippery slide. It was made from the same abrasive material and it was common for anyone using it to rip holes in their swimming costumes and often in themselves. Gran washed our grazes with stinging antispetic and covered them with band-aids. She had green and blue ones with stars on; we never had these at home.

After a long day of sun and swimming we'd head to the snack bar and spend our saved-up pocket money on icecream and lollies. This helped to reduce our appetite slightly and was an excuse not to eat much of Gran's cooking. When others reminisce fondly about their grandmother's cooking I smile and think of the lumpy porridge, incinerated roasts and poor, tortured vegetables cooked to a watery mush. But we survived, kids are resilient and being active and hungry helped.

Gran had a succession of boarders. Always elderly men who seemed to spend their days sitting on hard chairs in the closed-in front verandah. They had their meals in the dining room while we ate in the kitchen, so I never heard if they complained about the food. Some of them were there for many years so clearly they weren't finicky. One day I saw a boarder spring into action. Gorgeous hydrangeas grew next to the two front steps, and he leapt out the door to grab a big prickly brown grasshopper that was munching on a leaf. In front of my horrified eyes he ripped it in two and threw the corpse into the bushes.

These boarders were gossiped about in the street. Gran's neighbours two doors down, the Bakers, had kids about the same age as us and we got to know them well. We looked forward to seeing them every Christmas holidays. Mrs Baker often asked us about the accommodation arrangements and it was only years later I realised what she was hinting at. It makes me laugh to think of Gran having any sort of improper relationships with those old grey men. She was a model of morality, a strict Brethren. I'm sure she thought she was doing a service to humanity by offering her boarders a home. But I wish I'd discussed it with my mother – it's too late now. No, I can't picture Gran as a femme fatale.

She didn't have an easy adult life, working on a not very productive farm followed by a long period as a widow. Her German heritage was strong; she had a powerful faith and even more powerful sense of right and wrong. Although she was born in Australia, her German-heritage parents spoke a mixture of English and German which she sometimes slipped into. We usually worked out what she meant but I had to ask what 'ranching' meant. Turns out it's somewhere between drenching, rinsing and wringing and it's what happens to clothes in the laundry.

Gran's abysmal cooking was surprising, as her garden included a huge veggie patch. I remember cabbages, tomatoes, lots of herbs and prolific stands of peas and runner-beans. She did make one meal that I loved. Gran called it 'scritched eggs'. It was made with eggs from her own hens, broken directly into a hot pan onto a generous amount of melted butter. They were stirred up briskly, seasoned and a splosh of cream folded in. Then she threw in a big handful of chopped parsley. I can taste it as I write. Thanks for at least one good food memory, Gran, to add to the memory of a happy childhood.

LUCKY LOOKY

Miss Maggie shuffled to the stove and gave the cat a pat. He was a massive grey tabby of uncertain temperament called Looky. It seemed to me that he risked being roasted alive, but the old ladies said he loved the heat and moved away when the end he was curled up on heated up too much for his liking. It was a huge stove, a relative of the AGA, and varied in temperature from sizzling at one end to cat-comforting warmth at the other.

I say old ladies but they were probably only in their sixties when I was twelve. I'd known Miss Maggie and Lily all my life. They lived on the last farm in the mountains where Dad delivered fuel and orders from the town shops and collected cans of milk and cream for the butter factory. On Saturdays, because there was no school, I often went on the early morning run. I enjoyed all the farm stops, but Miss Maggie and Lily were my special loves.

It was mainly because they fed me; I was a greedy child. Miss Maggie was always wrapped in a padded dressing gown, tied tightly where her waist would be if she had one. She shuffled because she wore her brother's cast-off brown tartan woollen slippers, dragging rather than lifting her feet to progress. She'd reach into the bulging pocket of her dressing gown and bring out a handful of walnuts from the tree in the garden, or some powerful mints sent by a brother in England. I liked best the days she went to the pantry and came back with some savoury biscuits, shaped rather like fish. They were crisp and flaky and tasted vaguely of chicken but mainly of salty pastry. These biscuits, or crackers I suppose they were really, represented the height of sophistication to me who was used to Mum's gingernuts and jam drops. We never had savoury biscuits!

The kettle on the hot part of the stove would begin to sing, a sign for Lily to emerge from her room and supervise the tea-making. She was also clad in a dressing gown but wore her own well-fitting slippers, and was as thin and bony as her sister was round and comfortable. Her glasses, perched on the end of her nose, steamed up as she warmed the pot then poured boiling water onto the fragrant leaves.

This whole procedure was carefully timed and just as cups were being filled Dad would appear in the kitchen. He'd make himself a piece of toast, turning the thick slab of bread on its wire toasting fork over the flames in the firebox. Today he had a large box with him and I wondered what was in it. Nothing, it seemed, on closer investigation.

There was so much more to come on that dreadful and wonderful morning. When tea had been drunk and toast eaten Dad went to the stove and carefully picked up Looky. The cat was put unceremoniously into the box which the old ladies tied up firmly with string. The cat in the box was carried out to the truck and placed in the passenger footwell, so I had to sit with my feet resting on it. All the long drive home Looky yowled and cried and I cried a bit too, not being at all sure of his fate.

We turned into our driveway, and I finally asked Dad what was going to happen to Looky. I'd dreaded that he was going to be 'put down', a fate threatened to our own pets when they behaved badly. We were all animal-mad and didn't believe it would really happen.

'Why, he's coming to live with us, of course!' Dad said. 'Miss Maggie and Lily have sold the farm and have to move into town with their brother. They can't have pets, so they asked me to help find a home for him. He's pretty old now and it's best he goes to someone he knows.'

Surprisingly, Looky fitted into the household well and as we only had a small stove, he soon found his own warm spot on the hot water system.

The other day I came across the note Lily had written to accompany him, setting out his habits and food preferences. I realised that his name was actually Loki, after the Norse god of mischief. It figures; she was a classical scholar of some distinction.

MY GERMAN HERITAGE IS SHOWING

I recently wrote a very short story called 'A lesson from Grandma' about helping my Gran in the kitchen.(It was for a competition so I can't share it here, but I'll certainly let everyone know if it wins a prize.) Neither my Mum nor her mother were great cooks, so I don't look back with fond memories of lush meals. But they were both excellent at making some things; and one of Gran's specialties was sauerkraut. I quite liked it then and I've come to love it. Not all German food appeals to me but I regularly make sauerkraut, especially when cabbage is plentiful and inexpensive.

That's not really the case just now as fruit and vegetables are in short supply due to flooding of farmland. But I accidentally bought an extra sugarloaf cabbage, forgetting I had one in the fridge. Time to bring out the chopping board, salt and spices and start bashing away. Gran was born in Australia to immigrant German parents and spoke English which sometimes lapsed into a sort of pidgin German. She would instruct me to 'brash' the cabbage which I assume is a mixture of crush and bash. I still say it to myself.

I'll include the recipe separately. It's not completely traditional – we add a bit of dried chilli to the bottles to give a hint of heat. I use dried chillies from an Asian market – they are rich and dark with an almost caramel flavour. You can vary the spices to suit but the essentials are cabbage, caraway seeds and sea salt. I've never tried making it with alternative salt but if someone wants to try it, I'd love to hear how it goes.

You can make a version of kimchi – which I also love – by adding crushed garlic, a splosh of fish sauce, ginger, grated radish and extra chilli. Avoid cabbages with large, firm ribs; choose the leafy varieties.

It's important to start with perfectly clean utensils and hands so as not to contaminate the natural cultures found in the vegetables and atmosphere. Home made fermented foods are excellent for gut health, which has been found to greatly influence mental health. Bought, processed fermented products have been heat-treated to preserve them. This destroys a lot of the natural goodness found in the home-made products.

Be sure to use a large bowl sturdy enough to cope with pounding. I use the pestle from a granite pestle and mortar, but you can use a rolling pin, potato masher or the bottom of a clean bottle. You can just use your hands to squeeze and mash the cabbage but it takes longer.

If you haven't made it before you are in for a treat. I recommend making a small quantity (as in this recipe) to begin with until you are confident. There is a lot of tasting and estimating but if you follow the instructions all will be well.
There are many recipe variations available and you may want to experiment once you've mastered the basics.

Gran's Sauerkraut Recipe
(Leave out the chilli if you don't like spicy food)
Half a sugarloaf cabbage (about 750g)
  1 teaspoon each of caraway seeds, fennel seeds and peppercorns
2 cm piece of dried chilli, torn into small pieces
1 tablespoon of sea salt
1 small brown onion, finely sliced

Finely slice the cabbage, discarding the hard core and any tough or discoloured bits.

Place the sliced cabbage in the bowl and turn it over with your hands, separating it into shreds. This allows the salt and spices to penetrate well.

Add the salt and mix through. You can add the spices now or add them later, after the cabbage has been crushed.

Bash the cabbage well, for at least five minutes, until you can see some liquid at the bottom of the bowl. The cabbage will have reduced to about half the original volume.

Add the onion, spices if not added earlier, and chilli. Mix

together well.

Cover with a clean cloth and leave to stand for about 30 minutes.

With clean hands, squeeze the cabbage to help it release more brine.

Pack cabbage into clean jars and press down well. Leave about a centimetre at the top.

Pour in the brine until the cabbage is covered. If there isn't enough brine make some extra with pure water and salt – about 1 teaspoon salt to 250ml water.

Put on the lids and place jars on a tray to catch any liquid that might bubble out. Leave jars in a warm place – anywhere in the kitchen is usually good.

After a day or so you will see bubbles forming and coming to the top. Carefully open the jars to release pressure and push the cabbage down, making sure it is submerged. Do this every day for about five days. Taste it occasionally until it has reached the level of sharpness you prefer. I like it sharp but not too sour, usually five days is sufficient for my taste. You can safely leave it for up to ten days.

When your sauerkraut has fermented to your liking put the bottles in the refrigerator. It will continue fermenting but much more slowly. Check the bottles every couple of days and release the pressure.

Sauerkraut is good with rich stews or stirred into rice and vegetables. The famous Reuben sandwich is delicious and a good way to try it out.

LEAVING THINGS ALONE

I've always been a believer in 'leave things alone and they'll come right'. It's up there with 'turn it off and turn it on again', the standard advice from tech gurus.

Thinking here of the washing machine which I consider my greatest triumph so far. It's elderly, going on for twenty years old. It was absolutely the best model available when it first moved into my home. I know this because I sold them, I've visited the factory where they are made and studied comparison data with every model known to man.

I'm fond of it because it has dials and only one button that needs to be pressed to get it going. To be fair it's been moved three times in the last three years and hasn't always been set up on a perfectly level surface. So, when it recently refused to start washing and showed no signs of life I wasn't really surprised. It was worrying though, as I'd put detergent in the dispenser and the door had locked. After switching it off at the power point and waiting a few minutes it unlocked so I was able to retrieve my washing.

Not quite believing it would let me down so badly, I left it alone. But while 'down the shops' later I had a quick look at the local electrical store. Everything was, as expected, controlled by touch pads. At home later I switched the machine on and it proceeded to complete a cycle perfectly.

Two years later it's still going strong – only letting me down on two other occasions and responding to the same treatment - and I thank it every time it's used.

SHARING THE HOUSE

Probably the most unusal guests in my farmhouse were a family of Brush-tailed Phascogales. I spotted a little creature in the garden one evening just as the light was fading. It was busily collecting grassy mulch I'd put around the plants earlier in the day. It was quite a shock when it suddenly dashed over to the television antenna pole and climbed to the roof.

Then there was the pitter patter of little feet on the ceiling. Although it was more of a hop hop patter patter. The female phascogale – and I only worked out the gender later – had a mouthful of mulch to make a cosy nest.

There was just enough room under the corrugations on the roofing iron for this small marsupial to fit. Fortunately possums were too big to make their way in although they danced around on the roof, most nights, in hobnail boots.

I hadn't lived in the house long when I met the phascogales. A check-in with the previous owners confirmed that they had often seen them and, like me, were fascinated and delighted to have them visit.

Mrs Phascogale didn't confine her house visits to the ceiling. I'd set up my office on the closed-in verandah and often spotted her dashing about, not bothered by my presence or my small dog Ziggy. Ziggy had learned to leave visiting creatures alone and mostly just watched them with interest..

Soon there were more; three tiny, squeaking babies. They took over the house, falling asleep instantly in chairs, on tables and in shoes. At dusk they woke as if a switch had been flicked and tore about madly. They had no fear and if Ziggy or I were in their path they simply ran over the top of us. I learned to check every surface before sitting down or moving things – they slept peacefully through being handled and placed somewhere safer.

I watched them grow up and was sad when the whole family left. I saw them around the property sometimes and I'd like to think that the flick of tail they always gave meant they remembered me.

THE WHEATGERM CRUSH

It was my first real crush. He's never going to read this so I'll tell you his name – Alex Smythe. I was fourteen and he was twentyish and gorgeous. And I probably should have been charged with stalking; although I didn't know the word in the pestering context or would have been more restrained. Actually no, I probably wouldn't have been. It wasn't easy to negotiate my way into the same groups he attended at the church Easter camp. Our pastor seemed surprised when I signed up for advanced classes and discussions. He quietly murmured, as I filled in the attendance sheets, that I would possibly be bored and not understand the debates and dialogues. I ignored him. How could I be bored; I'd spend the hours gazing at the adored one's face, or the back of his head. It didn't matter which. A glimpse of his hand or hair was all I needed to fuel the passion.

With his long floppy blonde hair, penchant for double denim and a cute way of rolling his jacket sleeves to just above the wrist, Alex was unlike any of the boys from school or church. I was a passably attractive, unstylish early teen suffering from an overabundance of earnestness. I wanted to experience life with a capital L and mixing with visitors from other places fed my addiction.

Somehow I contrived to sit at Alex's table every mealtime, opposite him so I could continue gazing. Mum was helping with the catering and she seemed confused about my choice of seating.

'All your friends are over there,' she whispered as she refilled serving dishes and tidied away empty plates. 'Wouldn't you rather sit with them?'

'I'm meeting new people. It's so interesting hearing about their lives and experiences.' I knew Alex and his friends came from Brisbane so it was partly true. Their lives were so different; so exotic compared to my boring existence in a small country town.

My older sister Cath, who was supposed to be helping, overheard and sniggered noisily. I threw her a withering glance which she caught but ignored.

'Janey's infatuated with that blonde bloke. You won't shift her with a bomb.' Cath's voice was loud and carrying and I hated her. Alex didn't appear to hear; he was playing with his water glass – twirling it between his fingers. He had exquisite hands.

Please don't let him have heard and move away. I raised a silent prayer and tried to start a conversation with my neighbour, an older girl who clearly didn't think I was worth bothering with.

'It's lovely here on the mountain, isn't it,' I began. 'Have you been to camp before?'

'No, and I won't be coming again. This place is the pits. Segregated dormitories! How positively archaic.' She shook her glossy dark brown hair as if she were in a shampoo commercial and smiled artfully across the table.

Horrors. Alex was smiling back at her. He was probably just being polite. He couldn't fancy her. Yes, she was pretty, but I'd never heard her make an intelligent comment. I was sure Alex was more interested in a meeting of minds.

After lunch I went to find Mum in the kitchen. I wanted to borrow her new red trench coat to wear to the afternoon meeting. It had a sash belt that could be knotted at the back – a look I'd seen in fashion magazines. She wasn't there but Cath was, and she started on me at once.

'You are so transparent. Alex Smythe doesn't even know you exist; why would he bother with an infant like you?' She was always rubbing in her slightly greater age and experience. I knew I wouldn't win an argument so changed the subject.

'Do you know where Mum is? I thought she'd be here.'

One of the other volunteers spoke up. 'I think she's gone to have a rest. It's been so busy today and she's coming back to help with the evening meal.'

I went to the couples' quarters where Mum and Dad had a private room. Mum was there but not lying down. She was sitting on the bed putting on her walking shoes.

'I thought you'd be resting. Mrs Miller said you were.'

Mum looked up from tying her shoelaces. 'I had to get out of there. The noise level is deafening, so much chatter and clanging. I'm going for a walk in the bush – come with me?'

It was tempting as Mum was a great person to go walking with; she always knew the names of the plants and birds and saw things I missed. But I'd signed up for a talk on historical theology. I wasn't interested and had only the vaguest idea of what it actually was. I knew Alex was studying theology so that decided it.

'Love to, Mum, but I'm going to a theology lecture.'

She wasn't encouraging. 'I think you're a bit young for that, it's more for people who are studying to be a minister of religion.' Mum tried and failed to change my mind. 'And no, you can't borrow my coat, I want to wear it. It's cold outside.'

I headed off to the afternoon meeting to show Alex we were kindred spirits. Soon after the talk began, I knew it wasn't a great idea to be there. The speaker went around the room asking names and reasons for attending. I lied and said I believed I had a vocation to serve in the church. This attracted more attention than I'd expected, as I was not only young but female. In the sixties it was still a rarity for women to take an active part in the church. Apart from cleaning, catering and child-minding duties. And Alex wasn't even there to be impressed.

In my usual spot, perched on the hard bench across from him at the tea table, I summoned up courage to speak to him.

'That was a really interesting talk this afternoon; shame you missed it, Alex.' My voice quivered and I fought to keep it steady. 'I thought history of theology was one of your favourite subjects.'

Alex actually smiled at me. 'It is, but the man who took it is one of my lecturers at college and I've pretty much heard all he has to say on the subject.'

I nodded and tried to look intelligent. 'Did you do anything interesting?' I continued the interrogation.

'Went for a walk. Saw your Mum and we had a chat. She's an interesting lady.'

I died a bit inside. Surely Mum hadn't repeated Cath's remarks.

'She knows a lot about nature and the bush. I learned loads about local wildlife this afternoon.' Phew.

'I love nature too,' I went on, 'but didn't want to miss the talk.'

It was hard to get to sleep that night. 'If only' played over and over in my head.

At breakfast Alex brought out his personal wheatgerm supply and sprinkled it generously over his cereal. He sprinkled it over practically everything he ate. His assortment of vitamins and supplements was one of the things I found most fascinating. He'd explained the benefits to everyone at the table and I soaked up his words like a sponge. I was demonstrating a mature attitude to health that he would find attractive. I begged Mum to buy wheatgerm. I'd happily eat it and think of Alex. Next camp I could bring a matching stash.

Then it happened. The shampoo-commercial girl sashayed into the dining room and squeezed into the slight space next to Alex. He reached for her hand then leaned over and kissed her lightly. It was all I could do not to scream, the pain was unbearable. Of course Cath was watching. She moved into my line of sight and made eye-wiping gestures.

After forcing myself to swallow some toast I dashed off to find a private spot for a cry. Naturally Cath told Mum about what happened and Mum, always more aware than we gave her credit for, came to find me.

She didn't say anything at first, just sat beside me and gave me a hug. I leaned my head on her shoulder.

'I know, it hurts.' Mum said, surprising me. I'd been prepared for the lecture about how ridiculous it was to chase someone so much older. 'But better you found out early on that he wasn't interested. And now I don't have to buy wheatgerm and you don't have to pretend to like it.'

DREAMS OF SCOTLAND

The year before the Covid pandemic wiped out travel plans I made a trip to the United Kingdom. I'd been wanting to go for years and finally decided on a time. Previous visits had been only to London and then very brief stints working with chefs and catering companies developing menus to suit their kitchen equipment. It was airport to hotel to airport and home with no time for sightseeing.

I can't remember when I didn't have a love affair with Scotland. Originally the plan was to hire a car and drive around the whole of the UK but the friend who was to accompany me became too ill to travel. After much deliberation I selected a guided tour, something I never thought I would do, and it was wonderful. I loved every minute.

My favourite hotel was in the Cairngorms. We arrived just before dusk, a magical time of day. A photo of suitcases in a hallway was taken there, a random shot snapped as I left my room to go down to breakfast. I was pleased with the image and entered it in a photographic competition where it won a prize. It may have been the beguiling light or just the glorious highlands, but I was on a high for the whole time we stayed there.

Just down the road is Ardverikie House, the castle in the drama series *Monarch of the Glen*. A series that may have added to my passion for Scotland. And the very hotel we stayed in, Laggan Hotel, was used for some of the restaurant scenes.

I spent so much time outside gazing at the view my fellow travellers had to drag me indoors for dinner and the obligatory drink by the fireside. It was autumn so a fire was welcome. There were no other guests, we had the place to ourselves and were made to feel very welcome with every comfort provided and plenty of whisky.

Looking at the many photographs now takes me straight there

and I still feel the excitement of that brief stay. I'm definitely going back. Think I'll dig out my box set of MOTG right now and have another preview.

TO MALAYSIA FROM BRISBANE

It felt like paradise; the landscape we drove through was luxuriantly beautiful. The hotel was set in the middle of a golf course; all around were vast manicured lawns fringed with tropical gardens, dark green and spiked with colour. Once in our room we gazed and gazed out the window, occasionally turning to smile smugly at each other. Finally we gave in to the fatigue caused by the last few frenetic days and collapsed onto the bed to sleep.

The negotiations had been swift and simple, the hard part was sorting out our possessions, deciding which to leave, which to take with us. We had been advised to take whatever we wanted in the way of furniture and personal items, as it would be a long-term posting and we should feel comfortable with our surroundings. Lily had found a house that would probably suit, it had belonged to a diplomat and a few rooms were furnished with Chinese antiques. The floors were marble; it had five bedrooms and a tiny garden. She would arrange for us to inspect it, already I just knew it would be perfect.

So excited were we by our prospects that the last weeks in Brisbane flew past, with scarcely a moment for the promised get-togethers with family and friends. Nigel's fortieth birthday celebrations doubled as a farewell to some, and we *did* manage a last minute bon voyage party. Not everything went smoothly, the car hadn't sold and the house wasn't rented. We went directly from securing the last lock on the storage shed to the airport, shunning painful last-minute goodbyes. The thing was we just wanted to be gone, making a start on our new life.

This was not our first visit to Malaysia. Nigel had been every year for the last four years, and I had accompanied him once to a trade show, not knowing at the time that it was my first glimpse of a future home.

The flight was uneventful; we drank champagne and speculated on our future. At Subang airport the tropical heat hit us with a welcoming blast. Kahn and Lily from the company were there to meet us; they suggested we inspect 'the house' on the way to the hotel. It looked fine from the outside. The house had been closed up for weeks and the air inside dealt us another blast, redolent of damp and mould and rotting timber. On peering out of the upstairs windows we saw it overlooked sewage oxidation ponds. Two kitchen cupboard doors came off their hinges as we tugged them open, their fibrous innards spilling onto the floor. The marble tiled floor was buckled with damp, so were the swollen, powdery walls. The antique Chinese furniture was of the nasty, shiny, lacquered kind. We beat a hasty retreat, swearing never to return.

The next day we collected our temporary car, bought a street directory and proceeded to get lost. Navigating with directory in one hand, Malay-English dictionary in the other, I managed to guide us several times around but not into the city, missing every turn-off leading back to the hotel but almost finding Malacca. We soon got the hang of the Plaza Tolls, handing over the correct coins like old hands and practising our 'terimakasihs'. Unfortunately, it took much longer to get the hang of the expressways, with their bowel-like loops and rare, mysteriously sign-posted exits.

Back at the hotel, we staggered into the verandah bar and sank two large beers without speaking. The hotel was luxurious and comfortable, but miles from any shops or restaurants. We'd agreed we would find local food courts to eat in, but that evening we couldn't face climbing into the car again and indulged in room service.

The following day we found our way to the office to sign forms, discuss house-viewing and firm up starting arrangements. Instead of the promised two-week settling in period we were asked to start the next day, escorting an Australian consultant and his wife who were in Penang visiting an installation. Nigel realised Bob was an old friend from Sydney days, so we didn't really mind. We decided to have a break from practising driving in Kuala Lumpur, and lazed by the pool, mentally preparing for the long drive to Penang.

New colleague Ishan came with us, as navigator and local guide. The highway took us past rice fields, palm oil and banana plantations and the spectacular limestone peaks of Perak. I longed to see a rubber plantation and mentioned this to Ishan.

'But we have been passed lots already', he exclaimed.

'Well, point the next one out to me, I must have been asleep.'

'There, just coming up on the left, that's one.'

'Where, where, I can't see it.'

'There's another one ahead, on both sides of the road.'

I couldn't see plantations, only lots of straggly trees, but decided not to admit it. I'd identify them myself another time.

The road signs were in Bahasa Melayu. 'Ishan, what does 'ikut kiri kecuali memotong' mean?'

'*Ik-oot, ik-oot*', he snapped irritably. My sloppy Australian vowels always annoyed him. '*Ih-cat* means tie! The sign means something like 'keep left unless overtaking'.'

I tried to find the words in my dictionary but didn't yet know about the Malay suffixes and prefixes that make amateur translating a nightmare.

The hotel in Batu Ferringhi was a delight, so were the charming old houses surrounding it and the wonderfully colonial Penang Swimming Club nearby. Over dinner, we planned the next day's programme. Kahn, Bob, Ishan and Nigel would go off and do their boring business while Cheryl and I toured the island. I naively thought this would involve buses and guides but was informed it was too late to book tours and we would have to use one of the cars.

At breakfast, Khan stared at my toast, a look of disgust on his face.

'You can't eat that, it's as black as Ishan!'

I explained that it had taken three runs past the feeble toaster elements to arrive at this desirable shade.

'I'll never understand Westerner's tastes', he muttered,

loading his plate with sausages, baked beans, Danish pastries and fruit.

Nigel flung the car keys onto the table as the men assembled to leave for the day.

'Have fun, girls', they chorused. Cheryl and I lingered over our coffee. We had never met before, but I thought we'd get on well.

'You don't have to spend the day with me, you know. I was sort of pushed onto you, and I don't expect you to tag along with me if you'd rather be doing something else.' I was conscious that my liking of her might not be reciprocated, and anxious to give her an out.

'But I'm really looking forward to it. Where shall we go first?' Cheryl unfolded a tourist guide and spread it out on the table. 'There's a butterfly farm (not really), the botanical gardens (seen one, seen them all), Penang Hill funicular railway – now *that* sounds interesting.'

So, Penang Hill it was to be. A street map of Penang was kindly provided by the hotel. The car keys glinted at me mercilessly.

'I've never driven in Malaysia before', I confessed and added, with more confidence than I felt, 'and it's about time I did!'

A study of the map showed we had to head for Air Hitam. I couldn't resist showing off my brand new mastery of Malay. 'That's pronounced eye-er it-arm, you know. It means black water.'

In typical Malaysian style, the street sign spelling varied from Air Hitam to Ayer Itam, and I was thankful for the language and grammar cramming I'd done last night. Cheryl was a capable navigator, but something seemed to be going wrong. Despite following the map rigorously and turning into all the correct streets, we kept ending up at the botanic gardens. I was becoming rather flustered and light-heartedly suggested that perhaps that was where we were meant to go.

Cheryl was made of sterner stuff. She had already decided that the map was out-of-date, and on consulting the information officer, we learned that within the past year all the one-way streets in Penang had been reversed. You could, when you looked hard, see the faint painted-over arrows pointing in the opposite direction to the traffic flow. She threw the map into the back seat.

'We'll just look out for street signs; it shouldn't be too hard. What's that sign there say?'

It was one of the few words I knew. 'Awas, it means caution.'

'Well, I think you should use some awas and get over into the middle lane. There's a hill on the right that could be the one we're looking for.'

The next lot of signs confirmed this, and we were soon looking for a parking space at the foot of this very hill. Under the direction of a freelance parking attendant we squeezed in between two shiny Mercedes. He smilingly requested two ringgit for his assistance, and I gladly gave it to him. It was cheap for a whole morning's parking. On the way to the ticket office I saw the sign, luckily with an English translation: 'Parking RM2 per hour. Coupons available from information counter'.

The train was full and I was quite content to sit facing up the hill, admiring the stands of giant bamboo and watching the monkeys play on the wires. It really was very steep, and I was pleased to read a sign on the wall reassuring passengers that although the carriages were very old, the cables were inspected regularly. The ground fell away beneath us; I concentrated on looking up the hill and at the little groups of houses near the stations. At the top the air was cooler, it felt crisp and clean on our bare arms and faces.

A cool drink was the first priority, so we headed towards a hotel. I was distracted by the sound of birds overhead. Looking up, I spotted what appeared to be a kiosk on the very top of the hill.

'Let's go up there instead of to the hotel. It looks so picturesque.'

We wandered around the side of the hill, unable to find the road that led to the top. Taking a short cut through a cluster of buildings, too late we realised we had disturbed a group of Buddhist monks at prayer. We had failed to notice that the buildings formed a temple. Scurrying around the back, we surprised a monk at his ablutions. He quickly wrapped brown robes around his rotund body and bowed his head to us. We bowed back manically and fled cross-country up the hill.

A stroll through the precisely laid out rose garden restored our composure, until the storm broke. We had been too preoccupied to notice the gathering clouds and now dashed towards the building for a calming cup of delicious Chinese tea.

That evening, Cheryl recounted our adventures. 'It was brilliant,' she said.' I felt like something out of a Merchant Ivory film.'

We *had* looked rather theatrical, running through the rose bushes with our wild damp hair and clinging white linen frocks. We both declared that should it ever be required, we wanted to be put in the Penang Hill convalescent home with its exquisite English-style gardens and pure, healing air.

'No problems finding your way around, then?' asked Bob.

'None at all. We saw quite a lot of Penang, then went to the hill. After that we drove directly back to the hotel.' Cheryl's reply was technically correct, but I felt that the direct run back to the hotel was, on the whole, due more to chance than good management.

All I had wanted to do on returning to the hotel was find a bar and order the largest gin and tonic in the world. It seemed that driving in Malaysia was likely to lead to a dependence on alcohol.

COOKING FOR OTHERS 101

I've often wondered why Jill, a woman I know well and love, didn't cook at least occasionally vegan meals for her vegan daughter. I learned this a couple of years ago when I was invited to spend Christmas Day with the family and offered to bring food that that Joni could eat.

Jill scoffed at the idea, stating that Joni could bring her own food if she was too fussy to eat what was provided. Feeling rather smug, I arrived with a potato bake (soy milk, yucky vegan cheese and vegetable shortening) and a dairy-free, egg-free fruit cake. Both of which tasted fine despite the bland components. I also brought a tossed salad which interested no one. I nobly took a large portion because I actually like salad with roast meat and gravy. I was brought up on it.

Over the years it's become obvious that Jill never caters to anyone's preferences, her menus are the original 'take it or leave it' kind. I privately berated her for being an uncaring mother and friend. Only recently did I cut her some slack when it finally sunk in that Jill hates all cooking, always has and always will. She's provided for her family – they have grown up fit and healthy – but the cooking part has never been done with any interest or passion.

Home delivery food services were designed with Jill and her breed in mind. I can't think of anything worse but for her, they've been life enhancing.

CONNECTIONS

I often look back through my photographs. As a professional I study them carefully. What could I have done better? Was that setting or pose or lighting really the most suitable for the subject? One that surfaced recently is of Mrs Moran and Archie. Archie, a silky terrier, was well past his prime when I took the picture ten years ago. It wasn't the best idea to have him posed on a bentwood chair with Mrs Moran standing beside him. His rheumatism made it hard for him to sit on the small seat, a soft velvet cushion helped but his old body didn't look comfortable.

Other than that Archie was photogenic to a fault. His pointy ears and toothy grin gave him a jaunty air. Mrs Moran had tried her best but couldn't equal him. She faced up squarely to the camera; booted feet firmly planted, corsetted bulk held to attention. Nothing could help that unlovely face with its heavy features and downturned thin-lipped mouth. The bulky hat plonked on severely drawn back hair had a life of its own. Maybe the weight of yards of ruched fabric was responsible for the grimace. A silky fox fur slung around her neck did nothing to soften the overall effect.

It was not long after the war and Mr Moran, Sergeant Moran, hadn't come home. I surmised that life wasn't easy for Mrs Moran all alone on the farm. No children and only a farm hand for company. And Archie, of course. I wondered who those photographs were for. Possibly it was a tradition she couldn't bear to end. There had been too many endings for too many people.

Even now the photograph evokes a whiff of mothballs. I recall the scent of stale Eau de Toilette arising from the bulky woollen coat, securely buttoned against the icy wind. It looked like something you would put on to go out and feed the hens; not select for your annual portrait.

One large, capable hand clutched a furled umbrella; the other rested on the back of the chair, steadying it, she explained, against any sudden movements by Archie. Sudden movements were unlikely – his bouncing days were behind him. She said it was to keep the chair steady, but I suspect it was to keep a connection and maintain her upright stance.

I remember manufacturing a sneeze as an excuse to take out my lavender-scented silk handkerchief. Old dog, mothballs and stale perfume were a ghastly combination. When the exposure time finally elapsed I was thankful to dive under the cape. A new plate inserted, the timer set again for the second frame.

For some reason I kept the second print. The first one had been all that Mrs Moran wanted and something about that plain, rather forbidding lady and her ancient dog moved me. I was sad to see her funeral notice in the local rag last week. I assume Archie had gone long before her.

IT IS ENOUGH

It's enough that a blue-faced honeyeater
Came to the garden this morning.
Fog hid the distant peaks.
An old horse picked its way across the paddock,
Leaving green hoofprints in grass white with frost.

It was a joyless awakening, earlier.
The day held nothing new, no dreams or prospects.
Then a kangaroo came to the fence, peered over
Turned, bounding away to the creek.
It's enough. It will be good, this day.

DAD'S WAR

As remembered and written by his fourteen-year-old daughter

Our dad was in the war. I don't know who told us, or if we were ever told. Itas just part of life - it was there in his photo on the wall, mounted and framed in smooth polished timber with the insignia below and strange names engraved on brass: Halmakera, Biak, Moratai. We knew it *was* our dad because it said so on the plaque, and it looked a bit like him, only young. So young, that man with the strong features, smiling in a way that wasn't really a smile. A Mona Lisa look he has in that photograph.

'Dad, how important is a sergeant? Did you have stripes? Could you tell other soldiers what to do - did you make them clean their boots and march and salute? What did you *do* in the war?' Our knowledge of war was gathered from the papers and adventure books borrowed from the library.

Our mother gently interrupted our volley of questions. We hadn't known she was there, behind us.

'Your father doesn't like to talk about those days. It was a long time ago and he doesn't want to dwell on things that happened in the past.'

Reluctantly we ceased our questions, recognising the quiet voice of authority. But we kept on asking those questions to ourselves, we continued to worry and wonder. That the war happened a long time ago didn't seem like much of a reason for not talking about it.

Dad was a farmer *before* the war and sometimes it seemed as if he never stopped talking about those days. We knew it all by heart - the name of his favourite cows, how brilliant his quarter-horse was and how many ribbons he had won, how he managed to get a higher yield from the lower paddocks than anyone else in the history of the farm, and most of all about his life as a boy on the farm. When he was a boy children worked hard without being asked and were a help and comfort to their parents.

We, on the other hand, were idle, giggling, gossiping spendthrifts. We were only interested in having a good time, going off to friends' houses, going off to music lessons, swimming or the library. If we were at home all we did was listen to the radio or hide in a corner with a book.

Sometimes Dad forgot to lecture us and joined in our play. Our friends who witnessed this were most impressed by a father who volunteered to join our childish games of tennis or cricket. Our friends said that their fathers spent all their spare time lurking in work sheds or drinking beer. Our friends said we kids were lucky, but we weren't sure if we believed them. We suspected that our dad played games with us because he knew he could win if he wanted to.

So why couldn't our father tell us what he had done in the war? One day my oldest sister said a terrible thing. She said that Dad must have killed someone. She knew a girl at school who told her that her father had had to kill the enemy during the war, and he had gone very strange. He talked to himself and wandered off and got lost and had to be delivered home by neighbours or the police.

Our dad wasn't strange, at least not in that way. Although sometimes we had heard him yell out in the middle of the night and gone flying into his room fearing burglars or worse. Mum had shushed us and sent us back to bed.

'Your father had a bad dream and it gave him a fright, the old silly.'

We couldn't believe anything on earth, let alone a dream, could frighten our father enough to make him cry out in that dreadful way. Even the little ones didn't make noises in the night though they told us in graphic detail of the horrible nightmares they claimed to have had.

All of us agreed on one thing - that if our father had killed someone, he must have had a good reason. We couldn't really believe it, so we continued to wonder.

One Saturday, as on many Saturdays, I had invited some friends from school to work on a project at my house. They would stay for lunch and we would all go swimming in the afternoon. Our dining table was always crowded at weekend mealtimes, with tangled elbows and squashed up knees, lots of fooling around and laughter. Today, in addition to my school friends, we were joined by my older brother and sister's current romantic interests plus a couple of country cousins in town for a cattle sale. The table was a colourful chaos of squeezed in place settings, unmatched china and odd stools pushed into service as dining chairs.

Everyone but Dad was seated at the table and making a start on the cold meat and salad. Dad was working on some machinery in the yard and said not to wait for him. Soon we heard him washing his hands at the outdoor sink and the creak of the floorboards as he walked across the verandah. I had a new friend to lunch that day and was impatient to introduce her to Dad. I knew he would like her - she was clever and sensible and the stories of her family life kept me enthralled for hours.

'Dad, I want you to meet Mai. She's an exchange student from Japan. She'll be here for six months and I said she could stay with us for some of the time.'

Dad didn't sit down. He didn't even say hello. He said he had to finish the job in the yard and he would have his lunch a bit later. As he creaked to the back stairs I looked at my mother, worried that I had said or done something wrong.

'I would have asked first if Mai could stay, but you often let me have friends stay over. I didn't think Dad would mind.'

My mother looked at me - her eyes clear and direct. I knew that no falseness could ever lie behind that transparent gaze.

'Of course your friends are welcome to stay whenever they want. Your father just likes to finish a job properly once he's started. Now, let's clear the table and see who's got room for pudding!'

I knew Dad always finished what he started, but he had never, in my memory, missed a meal to do so. And how could he be so rude, especially when we had visitors? Feeling increasingly uneasy I looked around the table, but the tension had been dispelled by my mother's easy chatter. I decided to join in the general rabble and forget my father's behaviour. Grownups were hard to understand. Later that afternoon when I went to the refrigerator for some cordial, I saw his plated lunch carefully covered with an upturned bowl.

After dinner, an uncomfortably silent meal with bursts of loud, forced conversation from my mother and sisters, we were half-heartedly clearing the table and discussing our plans for the evening. Our father suddenly made a shocking announcement:

'Everyone please stay at the table for a few minutes. Your mother and I will clean up later.'

Dad was actually going to help with the washing up! Maybe he was going strange.

'Don't worry, I won't keep you long. I won't interfere with your precious plans.'

My older sister had begun to fidget. I knew she was panicking, thinking she might not have time to complete her beautifying routine before the boyfriend came back to pick her up. I had nothing planned that couldn't be delayed - just the usual Saturday night quarrel with my younger brother over the

Monopoly or Scrabble board. Dad looked to see that we were all seated, and then he began to speak.

'I know you are all wondering why I didn't join you for lunch today and left the room so suddenly. To tell the truth, I had a bit of a shock.'

That much I had worked out for myself. It was obvious that something had startled him, but I couldn't work out what it was. I guessed it was something to do with Mai, even though I had been so sure that Dad would like her. Briefly, the idea that it had something to do with her being Japanese flickered through my mind and was dismissed.

Dad continued, speaking quietly and not looking at us. His eyes were lowered to the table. This was almost as shocking as his offer to wash up. He always made a fuss about looking people in the face while you were speaking to them, being open and honest and so on, and he put it into practice especially when he was listing our multitudes of shortcomings.

'You children have often asked what I did during the war. I think it is time I told you something about it.'

Not now, Dad, tell us tomorrow or next week. Not now - you're upsetting our plans, spoiling our day, ruining our lives.... I could almost hear the unspoken words as my brother and sisters squirmed on their chairs. Dad looked up at us.

'I want you to know about one thing that happened to me during the war. You all know about prisoners-of-war and how badly the Japanese forces treated ours. Well, the Japanese prisoners-of-war weren't treated a lot better, but not many of them died in the camps from poor conditions. But - a lot of them still died before they reached home.'

Here it came, the revelation we had asked for. We didn't want to hear it. We didn't want to hear that our father had killed someone. We couldn't bear to know that.

'I didn't personally cause the death of any man, but sometimes I feel responsible for the deaths of many. You see, I was familiar with a lot of the islands north of Australia, so I was put in charge of a troop carrier which collected Japanese prisoners from the island prison camps and took them back to Japan when the war was over.'

His voice grew softer and began to waver. We leaned forward, scarcely breathing, straining to hear his words.

'Those men were so afraid of what would happen when they arrived home that they begged us to shoot them. Everyday I saw the terror in their eyes - many of them cried like babies. I tried to concentrate on all the stories I had heard about their barbaric fighting methods and how they tortured our own captured soldiers. I had a job to do and I did it, but never has doing my duty made me feel so sickened. I guessed that some of my men were providing means for the Japanese to take their own lives. God help me, I looked the other way.'

I felt the tears run down my face and drip onto my lap. I hadn't realised that I was crying. I looked at my mother and saw that her eyes were wet. The world had changed around me. I felt light-headed, unreal. If I reached out and touched my plate, I felt that my fingers would pass right through it. No one at the table spoke. What could we possibly say?

Dad drew himself bolt upright with a quick, familiar movement and his voice returned to normal.

'I want you all to understand just a little of what happened to me at lunchtime. When I came into the room and saw your new friend it was the first time I had come face to face with a Japanese person since the war. I know she is a child and has nothing to do with those times, but for a moment, she was one of the enemy. After a while, I calmed down and started to think more clearly. I pictured in my mind this alien person, enclosed and completely accepted by my family. I pictured her family. Maybe her father had gone through similar experiences. Some of the torment of the years began to seep away. It was wrong of me to keep the painful parts of my life from you. Today in my mind I accused you of being unfeeling and cold, introducing one of the enemy into our home, but how could you have known how I'd feel?'

It was a day for strange behaviour. Never normally demonstrative, I kicked back my chair and ran to my father. My arms went around his neck and I whispered, 'I love you Dad,' then bolted from the room. Somewhere in the dark night I had to find a refuge, a solitary place where I could quietly put together the pieces of my father's story. I knew that when the sun came up the next morning it would reveal a changed world. My world now held not only the innocence and joys of childhood but also the faintest hint, the smallest knowledge of a grown-up pain.

THE RED BOOTS

I love red shoes and have owned many pairs. A photo on my phone shows my favourite red boots on the stony beach at Lynmouth in Devon. It was a day filled with emotion as I visited the town where my father's family lived, three generations ago before migrating to Australia.

There are still relatives there but I didn't get to meet any on that trip. Those boots walked many miles around the UK and they are still going strong. It was a lovely autumn day, fresh but not cold. The previous day I'd trekked around Dartmoor and towns in the south and it was cold, wet and windy. Delicious. Just what I expected.

I didn't get to Hoar Oak cottage which had been my main destination, as recent severe storms had turned the tiniest streams into raging torrents. I didn't like my chances of jumping lightly over them on the hike. There will be another visit and I'll get to visit the little house that has sheltered several families of farmers, mainly shepherds. My great-great grandfather Josiah was the last of my family to live there.

The next red boots are my current gumboots, and they have been well-used lately. It's been wet in this part of Australia. My home town has been cut off several times by floodwaters but unlike many areas, no dwellings have been inundated. It's a lesson that we should be taking better care of this beautiful planet.

The cottage is in the valley behind me in the last photo. I imagined the roaming sheep and farm workers toiling up and down that hill.

http://hoaroakcottage.org/

I REMEMBER THE WALK

I remember the walk – a good mile – a long walk for young legs. Some days I called in at my friend's place in the next street, but often she wasn't ready and her mother would drive her later. I didn't have a chauffeur; my dad was at work by then with the family car. Sometimes a neighbour would offer a lift if it was raining hard, but mostly I was happy to walk to school. I walked that path, with deviations, twice a day for seven years, and every day there was something new to see.

On frosty winter mornings there were silver cobwebs in the long grass. My breath fogged, I pretended to smoke a wicked cigarette. The icy, crunchy short grass soaked through my polished-every-morning shoes. Only the school street had a proper footpath, mostly I walked on the wide grassy strip between the road and the front fences.

Spring brought new flowers to all the gardens. Every morning I checked out the new buds, and chatted to friends and neighbours. Most afternoons there was a bunch of flowers, a plant cutting or a basket of peas or strawberries to take home for Mum. I sat on the edge of the road and looked at the sky – wispy clouds dashed about against an unbelievable blue. Puddles in the grassy drains were teeming with tadpoles, fodder for school projects. What joy when their little legs began to grow, and what sadness when they hopped to freedom in the night.

Soon it would be time for the Show. Remember to go to school the other way, it was dangerous to walk past the show grounds once the show (carnival) people arrived. This made them irresistible, and I yearned to meet them. I walked defiantly by the forbidden grounds and saw a monkey in a cage, right near the fence. He bit me viciously as I tried to make friends, and I couldn't confess the cause of my wound.

In summer the magpies and butcher birds sang high above my head. I dashed past the park where they nested, other kids told horror stories of blood pouring from gashes in their heads where they had been pecked by crazed birds. But the magpies never bothered me, perhaps because I never bothered them. I loved to listen to the monotonous chee-chee call of the babies, and the soft gurgle as food was pushed into their gaping mouths.

The liquidambar trees in the church yard turned golden brown, fallen leaves crackled underfoot and I knew it was autumn. It turned briskly cool in the mornings, and the days began to shorten, the sun was setting in a misty golden haze as I arrived home late after music lessons.

The smell of burning leaves filled the air, smoke rose from every backyard. We played bonfires, Joan of Arc groaned horribly as the flames licked at her legs.

The end of primary school was the end of an era of private discoveries. It was hard to breath in the change of seasons in a high school bus with forty others. It was time to explore another world, a world of scholarship and growing up.

I'M WORRIED I'M AN INTELLECTUAL

Channelling Adrian Mole.

I don't find talking about the weather interesting if It's about clothes drying on the line. Or not drying.

Yes, if it's about plants and animals dying. Or the damage people are doing to the environment. But that's climate, not weather.

Yes, if it's about being able to drive to the city to meet a friend for lunch or attend a concert and not get hailed on or have to negotiate flooded roads. Or being able to keep an appointment with my hairdresser. These things are important to me. So I'm not an intellectual.

Intellectuals are rational people who don't worry about things they can't change. So I'm not an intellectual.

THE SMOKE EFFECT

With several countries legalising the growing and using of cannabis lately (not smoking but food and medicinal) I've been reminded of something that happened while I was in Switzerland many years ago. It's still illegal to supply cannabis there but some cantons allow a small quantity to be grown for personal use. In the small town where I was working a colleague told me the local policeman had given him some plants of exceptional quality.

It was a joy to travel for work and to share in workmate's lives. One evening my partner and I, along with several others from the company, were invited to an archery session and dinner at a place in the country. The long twilight was lovely as we drove past orchards and beautiful gardens, finally arriving at a house in the hills. I'd never tried archery and found it quite challenging but managed to acquit myself reasonably well.

There was a large teepee in the front yard, something I'd noticed in a few places. After dinner we took our glasses of wine into the teepee and our host, Stefan, made a fire in the middle. It was soon rather smoky although a lot of the smoke found its way out through the hole at the very top.

We were all pretty happy: chatting, telling stories and even bursting into song. I surprised everyone, and mainly myself, by giving a word-perfect rendition of *The Gambler*.

Suddenly one of the young staff chefs stood up and demanded quiet. 'Listen. Just listen.'

'What are we listening for?' someone asked.

'Can't you hear it? Thud, thud, thud. Something sinister is coming, I can feel it!' He became quite agitated and took himself outside to check on the approaching monster.

When he hadn't returned after a few minutes I went out to check on him. He was lying on the ground under an apple tree.

'It's wonderful here. The apples are falling all around. So peaceful.' He was perfectly content so I left him there and went back to the others. The fresh air had made me a bit woozy although I had had very little to drink.

'He's fine,' I reported back to the others. 'But has he been taking something? He seems a bit out of it.'

Stefan looked sheepish. 'Could be the smoke,' he suggested. 'It has that effect on some people.'

Finally he admitted that he'd cut back his cannabis plants recently and had been burning the prunings.

We all went outside then and breathed deeply of the clear, pure air until we felt composed enough for the drive back to town.

YEAR OF THE RESOLUTION

I've made my resolutions and I'll stick to them like glue
Number one is easy but then so is number two.
More time for friends and family proudly heads the page
The one that follows on ensures that even in old age
I'll be around to do just that, I'm full up to the brim
With dread and dedication; I've signed up for the gym.

The one that follows on is simply known as number three:
Every time I light a fire I'll plant another tree.
Number four is founded on a personalised bent
It's time to give up whisky, but I'll save that one for Lent.
Of course, of course, I'll walk much more; it hardly need be said
That every time I make a snack I'll pass on the white bread.

And this year just could be the one I get down from the shelf.
Does he exist, this creature rare who fits with my good self?
It could be time I listened to my friends' impassioned pleas
And *tried* at least to find a bloke who'll end up my main squeeze.
This leads to other issues that need to be addressed
With grooming, style and fashion I will strive to keep abreast.

That brings my resolution count square up to number ten

And that's enough for anyone, I'm calling up a zen

Moment or two to mull on through my challenges this year,

I swear to you and cross my heart – to all I will adhere.

    It's good to know for certain that this year will roll on by

My list will still work next year when I'll have another try.

DREAM V1 (AFTER SEEING A TRAFALGAR TRAVEL NEWSLETTER ABOUT CHEAPER SINGLE SUBSIDIES)

We – a tour group - were somewhere in the north of Africa or the Middle East. There seemed to be a lot of sand which looked like a desert. The path was made of rough pavers unevenly pressed down into the loose sand. Every hundred metres or so there was a big step up, so high I had to put my hands down to gain enough leverage to make the leap. The others were getting further and further ahead and soon they disappeared out of sight. I wasn't too worried. I had plenty of time to meet the bus and this was the only path. Wrong. After negotiating a particularly high ledge the path divided into two, and soon after it divided again.

I opted for the lowest paths, thinking they would be more likely to lead to the bus station. Eventually I reached a sort of shed made of timber with a tin roof. There were two women sitting on a bench inside. I went to sit down near them and one of them turned to me and hissed. She had a scarf knotted around her head in the particular style adopted by the local women. Surely she hadn't really hissed at me? The locals had seemed so friendly. Then both of them were making hideous faces and hissing. Enough, I could take a hint. I went outside and saw there were buildings all around which I hadn't noticed on my approach. So I was close enough to civilisation for my mobile phone to work and I could check the way to the bus depot. There had been no phone service on the long hike.

Where was the phone? Not in my capacious shoulder bag, nor in any of my pockets. I emptied my bag onto the ground and checked the lining and internal pockets. Then I saw the phone on the ground, a little way away. How it got there I didn't bother to think about, I just knew it was mine. But it was different. It was my phone but a completely different model with strange buttons and screen. I tried to find my contacts as bizarrely, even though I didn't know the phone, I believed it was mine and would have all my familiar apps and features.

Those women must have swapped my real phone for this one – they were the only people I had been near enough to. As I was deciding to walk to the buildings they faded away but I saw my friend Suzy walking towards me. She would help, she would have a usable phone. She hadn't been on the bus trip but happened to be in the area. So fortunate.

The story had a positive ending so not the usual travel anxiety dream.

IN THE YELLOW HOUSE

I was happy

That sunny Sunday.

Pools of light lay

Golden on the floor.

I was happy

Alone, in the house.

Silent and still.

Then music, it was Mozart.

The mighty Jupiter

Leapt and filled the room.

My heart surged

With unbearable joy.

The street dreamed on.

Soft breezes played

And palm fronds danced

With a gentle beat.

I looked through

Filmy curtains, they

Stirred so gently.

Filtering the view,

Changing the light

Stippling the walls.

I was happy, that Sunday

At the window.

I watched, with yearning.

I was almost happy

That Sunday, alone.

THE MEETING

Olivia lowered herself into a deck chair and stared out to sea. She had to admit the view was stunning, the best thing about the house. Today a breeze was whipping up white tips on deep blue waves, small boats flaunted a rainbow of coloured sails as they came in sight around the end of the harbour wall. The sun was high in the sky. She should have covered up; put on a hat and Factor 50. She'd inherited her father's carroty hair – it couldn't be called anything as glamorous as auburn – and pale, freckly skin that burnt in minutes. She grabbed a towel from the chair beside her and slung it around her shoulders.

Tim was out there somewhere, pretending to be a seasoned sailor when he'd only had the boat for five minutes and relied on his mate Robert's knowledge to keep them afloat. Naturally he had to buy a boat and enter the annual regatta, if only to show the Scarborough community he was a man of the people. Tim wouldn't be worrying about sunscreen, his olive skin tanned quickly which heightened his striking good looks. His eyes seemed even bluer against a tan and his wavy dark hair developed attractive streaks. Olivia didn't want to think about Tim. She wasn't sure if she hated him or was mad about him. She knew she was mad *at* him.

Once the estate agent had shown her and Tim the house he had to have it. They needed to move out of their small flat in the city and find something bigger, that had become obvious. Tim had talked her into buying – Olivia would have been happy to rent for a bit longer while they looked around and found something more affordable. Houses on the waterfront were a ridiculous price. Tim said his legal practice was going well, he'd always wanted to live near the sea, and it would be a good investment. People always agreed with Tim, and it had become a habit for her, too. He would be an asset to the district; he should be on the local council. At least that's what everyone said and Tim had aspirations in that direction.

Why had she chosen that chair, Olivia wondered. She'd never get out of it. She wriggled it over to the edge of the verandah and scrambled up the railings. Having succeeded in coming to an upright position she leaned on the rickety handrail and hoped it would support her weight. It needed painting, flakes of paint stuck to her skin and she peeled them off in disgust. The small amount of effort had brought her out in a sweat which she detested. She loathed being pregnant.

She'd been excited for about a minute when the doctor confirmed her condition. Secretly she'd hoped that being a few weeks late and feeling tired were symptoms of the tummy upset that had bugged her for a while. They should have used extra protection; she knew the pill wasn't reliable after you'd been being sick. She should have insisted Tim use a condom but she didn't need the argument. He was ready to start a family. It didn't matter if one of his little swimmers found its target - he was thrilled to learn one had. The arrival of Tim Junior would be just what they needed to settle them down in their new house. He was ready to be the devoted family man.

Olivia wished they hadn't learned they were having a boy. She could have gone on hoping it would be a girl. Being pregnant was bad enough. She didn't think she could cope with another Tim.

Maybe his boat would capsize. That wouldn't help, Tim was an excellent swimmer. She didn't really want him to drown, her emotions were all over the place. Hormones, everyone said. Both her doctor and her best friend Imogen said it was normal to have unusual thoughts and strange fancies. So far Olivia hadn't had a craving for anchovies with ice cream or pickles with everything, which is what Imogen said she had. Olivia chose what she ate more carefully than usual. She wasn't a brilliant cook and had always preferred plain food. Tomato sauce on toast was as weird as it got. If she was going to have a baby, and it seemed inevitable no matter how much she wished it away, it would at least be healthy and well-nourished.

Which led her to think of her other fears. What if there was something seriously wrong? Like Fragile X syndrome or missing limbs. She'd had all the tests and so far, at eight months, no indication of anything to worry about. It didn't stop her worrying. Most nights, while Tim snored gently beside her and she tried not to disturb him by aimlessly trying to get comfortable, she reached for her iPad and consulted Dr Google. She couldn't work up any enthusiasm about becoming a mother but she was organised. Sandy, her employer, had suggested a baby shower instead of a leaving do and she'd agreed. It would have been nice to have a party just for her though. It seemed everything from now on would be about the baby.

'Lovely day for the regatta!' Pat from next door was leaning over the fence trying to catch her attention. 'How about we go down to the jetty and watch from there. They should be coming in soon.'

'Thanks, but it's a bit hot for me.' Olivia didn't think she had the energy to stay standing, let alone walk down to the harbour. All she wanted was to find somewhere comfortable to sit, preferably with a long cool drink.

The front gate creaked open and clanged shut. Now Pat was coming up the stairs. 'Why does she have to butt in. The house is a mess and I can't cope with visitors.' That wasn't a fair thought, Pat had never been pushy. She'd made a cake to welcome her new neighbours and then left them to it. In fact, she was the ideal neighbour, friendly but not intrusive. Now she had barged in, uninvited.

'You look done in, lovey. Come inside and I'll make you a cuppa.' Pat had taken her arm and was guiding her into the cool depths of the house.

'I'm fine, thanks. I don't need anyone to look after me.' Olivia knew she was being rude but she had to put Pat off. She hadn't cleared away the breakfast dishes or wiped down the bench. And she knew she looked a mess – she hadn't brushed her hair properly or worn makeup for ages.

'Actually, I think you do. I'm not judging, I know how hard it is to cope at this stage. And you're such a tiny thing. I've always been hefty and I struggled when I was carrying the kids.'

Olivia collapsed onto a sturdy kitchen chair. The bin needed emptying, the sink was full of dirty dishes; the kitchen was a tip. She couldn't cope with anything lately, let alone housework. She realised she was crying. Not sobbing but letting the tears run down her cheeks, into her mouth and dripping onto her blouse.

Pat put a glass of water and roll of kitchen towel on the table, then carried on filling the kettle and poking around for mugs and teabags.

'Thanks. Sorry.' Olivia mopped herself up and took a sip of water.

'It's fine. I was the same. How do you take your tea?' Pat was pouring boiling water onto English Breakfast teabags. Olivia had avoided caffeine for the last few months and stuck to peppermint or camomile, neither of which she actually enjoyed. A cup of real tea sounded wonderful.

'Just a bit of milk, please. You *are* kind.' Olivia swallowed hard to stop herself crying again. 'There are some biscuits in that tin. Not homemade, I'm afraid.'

Pat plonked the tin on the table between them and eased off the lid. Olivia's mother would have been shocked to see them eating biscuits from the tin. She insisted on matching cups and saucers, serving and side plates. Milk in a jug, sugar in a bowl.

'How many children do you have? Where are they?' Olivia was suddenly curious about this nice woman who seemed to have taken over her kitchen.

'Two, a boy and a girl. And they each have one of each as well. We're a very neat family.' Pat smiled at the thought of her grandchildren. 'Jason lives in Singapore and Penny's in Melbourne. I don't get to see much of them. Thank heavens for Facetime.'

'What about your husband? I assume you have one. Or had one, at least.' For someone so keen on privacy Olivia realised she was being rather personal. 'Sorry, you don't have to tell me. None of my business.'

Pat put down her mug and reached for a biscuit. 'It's okay, not a secret. Yes, there was a husband but he decided being a family man wasn't for him, at least not with me. Penny was only two when he buggered off so it's really just been me and the kids.'

'Mum and Dad helped a lot,' Pat continued. 'I had to go back home for a while when Bob left. Couldn't have managed without them.'

'My Mum's coming to stay in a couple of weeks. If she can be spared from the shop.' Olivia's mother ran a trendy boutique in North Sydney. It was debatable how much help she'd be, Olivia thought. She'd criticise the state of the house, her clothes, her cooking. She wouldn't criticise Tim though. She made no secret of the fact she thought Olivia had been lucky to marry someone so attractive and charismatic.

'That's good, love. You'll need your Mum. And your dishy husband – will he be taking time off work?'

So Pat had fallen victim to Tim's charm too. 'He said he'll work from home for a while. I don't know how much help he'll be though.'

'You'd be surprised. It's obvious he adores you. You just need to tell him exactly what you need him to do; he may not work it out for himself.'

Pat continued, 'The best thing he can do is take over some of the feeds and housework and let you rest.'

'That's what my friend Imogen said. I'll talk to him about it.' So Pat thought Tim adored her! Maybe he did. She hadn't been very adorable lately. It was hard, she was furious about today.

'I really wanted him to stay with me today but he insisted on taking that stupid boat out.' Olivia couldn't keep it to herself any longer. 'I told him I was feeling strange. I had such a bad night and couldn't settle down.'

'Why are you looking at me like that?' Olivia noticed a frown appear briefly on Pat's face. 'You think I'm selfish, don't you.'

'Not at all. Just remembering something. Another cup?' Pat picked up their mugs and switched the kettle on. 'It's normal to feel uncomfortable. I'm sure your doctor told you that. And you've had a busy time what with moving house and sorting out things for the baby.'

'I didn't want to move. I didn't want a baby!' Olivia was crying again. 'I loved my job in the bookshop. It wasn't a brilliant career, but I was happy there.'

'So the little one wasn't planned. You don't want kids?' Pat had moved over and was massaging Olivia's tightly knotted neck and shoulders.

'I do but not yet. I wanted to have more time with just us. But Tim can't stop talking about the baby. He even calls him Tim Junior.'

'Oh Pat,' Olivia was really sobbing now. 'What if I don't like the baby. What if he doesn't like me! Sorry for blubbing, I don't know what's happening to me!'

'You're having a baby, that's what. And if my memory serves me right it may be sooner than you think. Is it the birth that worries you?'

'No, that's not the problem. I'll just be glad when it's all over. But it won't be, will it. There'll be someone else here all the time.'

Olivia's phone was ringing – she'd left it on the verandah. 'Do you mind answering that, Pat. Not up to talking to anyone just now.'

Pat collected the phone and brought it back into the kitchen. 'It's Tim; do you still want me to answer it?'

'Yes please.' Olivia couldn't trust herself to speak to him.

'Hi Tim, it's your neighbour Pat here. Olivia's having a bit of a rest.' Pat had moved into the next room and Olivia strained to hear her side of the conversation. 'I think it would be a good idea if you came home. I have a feeling there's going to be some action here soon.'

'What are you talking about? What did he say?' Olivia had lurched to her feet and was reaching for the phone.

'He said he was going for a drink with the others and would be home later this evening. I hope I persuaded him to come straight home.' Pat handed the phone to Olivia. 'Think there's a new text message, too.'

'It's from Mum. She's not sure if she can make it now and she's sending some more stuff for the baby.' Olivia wasn't sure if she was upset or relieved, probably a bit of both. 'She *has* been generous. Tim's made the nursery gorgeous; between them they've taken it over. He even painted the walls himself - a lovely creamy yellow.'

'So he's excited about the baby then?'

'He can't wait to be a father. I think it's because he doesn't have any family of his own. He was brought up in care and never been able to trace his birth mother.' Olivia felt a surge of love for her dishy husband. They'd talked about it and now suddenly it became clear why he was desperate for a blood relation. She moved to the window to watch for him.

'Oh bugger, Pat, I've wet myself.' Just when she was feeling calmer this had to happen. In front of Pat, too.

'Don't think that's pee, lovey. I'd say your waters have broken. Got your bag packed?' It was just as Pat had suspected. This baby was ready to make its entrance into the world.

'All set, checked off the list last week. Imogen helped me. Do you think we should wait for Tim?'

'No, I'll get my car out and drive you to the hospital. You have a freshen up and change and I'll be back in a minute. You can phone Tim and your doctor on the way to the hospital.' Pat didn't want to take any chances. Even though this was a first baby things could still happen quickly. 'You are planning on a hospital birth?'

'Definitely, yes. All organised.' Olivia was starting to feel nervous. Not scared exactly, but apprehensive. And a bit excited too.

'Won't be long. I'll be back soon and help you down the stairs.'

But Olivia was waiting at the foot of the stairs when Pat drove the car into the driveway. She'd packed a few essentials too – no knowing how long she might be at the hospital. There was no sign of Tim. He could go straight there if and when he decided to leave the pub.

Tim arrived at the hospital hours later. As he was leaving the pub he remembered switching his phone off to save the battery after calling Liv earlier. A jumble of voicemails and texts announced themselves and he worked through them. Luckily he hadn't had much to drink; he'd been more interested in rehashing the race with everyone in the bar. But he wouldn't risk picking his car up from home; an Uber would be safer.

There was nowhere open to buy flowers so that could wait until tomorrow. The receptionist directed him to Olivia's room, on the way he nipped into the men's room to wash off some of the salt and tidy himself up. He'd been looking forward to a hot shower and early night but now he was full of energy – adrenalin boosted.

A woman was going into Olivia's room. Didn't look like a nurse or doctor. Might be the neighbour – Pat something. She was carrying takeaway cups and he hoped she had a spare coffee for him.

'Hi Tim. Better late than never, I suppose. Olivia's asleep. She's had a couple of contractions but the midwife doesn't think she'll go into labour proper for a few hours yet.' Pat was ready to hand over the bedside vigil. It was late and she wasn't as young as she used to be. 'There's a coffee for you if you want it, looks as if you could use one.'

'Thanks. You've been very kind. You must be ready for your bed.' Tim sank into a hard chair and stared at his wife. She looked very small and fragile. A blue hospital sheet was pulled up to her chin.

'It's been a bit of a day all right. But everything is fine and happening as it should. I'll be off now. Give me a call when you have some news.' Pat picked up her bag. 'My number will be on your phone from when I sent a text before. Your phone charger is in Olivia's bag – she thought you might need it.'

'Thanks so much. Just one thing; how come you were at our place this afternoon? Did Liv call you?'

'No, I was out the front watching the boats and we got talking. She looked tired and a bit pissed off so I tried to make myself useful.'

Lucky I did, Pat thought to herself. But then he couldn't have known what would happen – apparently the due date was three weeks away.

'I'm really grateful. She would have been frightened on her own. I probably wouldn't have been much use either,' Tim was willing to concede. 'But I'm here now and not going anywhere.

Pat was already at the door, 'I'll let them know at the nurse's station that you're here; the midwife can bring you up to speed.'

Tim watched his wife. Olivia hadn't been sleeping much lately and he'd been worried. He knew she was anxious about the baby but he'd been more concerned about her. She'd need all the rest she could get before their son arrived.

A soft tap on the door startled him. The midwife beckoned him into the corridor. 'Let's not disturb Olivia just now. She seems very tired so let her sleep while she can. I don't expect anything to happen tonight and the buzzer is right near her hand.'

'What should I do?' Tim was hyped up, ready for action.

'Nothing you can do for now. Better try to sleep as well. Did you bring any night things?'

'I came straight from the pub, Mrs Baldwin. We were commiserating after not winning the regatta.'

'I'll get someone to bring you pyjamas and a towel. A nurse will call in to check on your wife but use the call button if you need to.'

Showered, coffee-infused and feeling more composed, Tim resumed his bedside vigil. The spare bed looked inviting but he was afraid he might not hear Liv if she called for him.

'You're going to have a terrible crick in your neck.' His wife's voice woke him from a heavy sleep. She was right, his head was resting at a strange angle on the edge of the bed. He painfully attempted to straighten it.

Olivia was trying to sit up. 'Help me up, I need a pee.'

'Are you okay? What do you want me to do?' Tim was wide

awake now.

'I'm fine, I think. Just need to go to the bathroom.'

Tim looked at his watch – just gone 2am. Olivia climbed out of bed and headed for the ensuite.

'Could you make me a cup of tea please, Tim, there's a kitchen just down the hall. And see if you can find something to eat.'

Olivia was sitting up in bed when Tim returned with tea and a stash of cellophane wrapped biscuits. She had combed her hair, put on lipstick and was calmly applying hand cream.

'Great, I'm starving. They gave me some sandwiches but I didn't have much to eat all day yesterday.'

Tim watched as Olivia carefully dunked a gingernut. 'Actually, should you be eating? What did the doctor say?'

'I'm having a baby, not surgery. Nobody said anything about not eating.'
Olivia demolished one pack of biscuits, reached for another and gasped. 'Think we'd better call someone though – I've just had a contraction.' She pushed the bed table away and pulled her knees up to her chest.

Suddenly the room seemed to be full of people – he realised later it was just Mrs Baldwin, a nurse and briefly, a doctor. Tim did as he was told, donning a mask and hospital gown and taking up his position at his wife's side. She was perfectly calm now and he went through the routines they'd learnt at the antenatal classes. They'd been shuffled off to a delivery ward before returning to the private room. There were three of them now – a family.

Pat arrived just after 10am. Tim had forgotten to phone her and jumped up guiltily.

'Stay there, I've just come to drop off some things for you both.' Pat was loaded up with coffee, bacon rolls and an overnight bag. 'I've put in some toiletries and a change of clothes for you, Tim. Hope that's alright. Olivia told me to keep hold of the key when she locked up yesterday.'

'It's more than alright, it's wonderful. I've only got these dirty, sweaty things.' Tim had been dozing on the bed. He looked over at his sleeping wife.

'I see his nibs is looking pretty perfect.' Pat bent over Olivia's bed, putting a gentle hand on the little bundle tucked in beside her.

Olivia opened her eyes and looked up at her neighbour. 'I think we all did a good job.'

'You were amazing,' Tim took up the story. 'I didn't do much except get in the way. It all happened so quickly. I thought it would take much longer.'

'He was in a hurry to meet you both.' Pat reached for a tissue from the box by the bed. 'Now I'm blubbing. I'm just so happy for all of you. When can you come home?'

'Some time today, I think. The doctor will be around later to check all is going well, which I'm sure it will be.' Tim searched in his pockets and handed his car keys to Pat. 'Would you mind picking us up? I'll let you know what time once Liv has the all clear. Lucky I fitted the baby capsule last week, didn't think it would be needed so soon.'

'Could I have a cuddle, do you think?' Pat looked down at the baby, who now had his slaty blue eyes wide open. 'Is that okay with you, new mother?'

'Of course. I'd be shocked if you didn't want to.' Olivia gave Pat a shy smile. She knew they were both thinking about yesterday's conversations. It seemed so long ago now.

'It's fine Pat, really. Now that we've met I think we are going to be just fine.'

THE KING AND I

I was used to being peered at through the french doors and woken by his unmusical call; he would sit on the chair on my verandah and heckle me until I gave in and fed him. Not at the normal feeders, but on his special plate on the table, along with my own breakfast toast and coffee.

Australian King Parrots are indisputably special and they know it. A regular family group visited for breakfast and dinner every day, with sometimes a few friends along. The male in particular seemed to like company and stayed close by for hours at a time, calling from his treetop vantage point until I acknowledged him with a return whistle. By the amount of food the parent birds were putting away, I realized there was a baby at home.

The day came when I had to leave the farm for a six-month stint overseas. My partner had gone ahead, I wanted to close up the place and spend the last day there by myself, revisiting my favourite places and being emotional without witnesses.

As I was giving the shed a final check and locking it up, father King swooped down at me then landed on a nearby post. I made a final round of the new trees, checking the watering system and pump; all the while he kept circling me. We went back down the track to the house together, with him swooping in front and landing close by repeatedly, as if to make sure I kept going in the right direction. This was unusual behaviour, but I didn't try to analyse it at the time.

Arriving at the house he did a few more swoops then went to the tree overhanging the clothesline. There sat his wife and baby son. I'm not one to romanticise the actions of wild creatures, but I couldn't help thinking he had wanted me to see his offspring before I left. We sold that farm a couple of years later and lots of Australian King Parrots visit the new property, but I've always remembered the bond I felt with that bird, on that day.

DREAM V2

I was standing outside a house where apparently I was living. There was a huge part of the side wall missing. I looked down at my striped flannelette pyjamas which were torn and dirty. There seemed to be something else wrong but it wasn't immediately obvious.

A few people came up to me including my partner. Where he came from I have no idea, he was just milling around with the others.

'What happened?' he asked. 'Why are you outside the house and not dressed properly.'

'There was some sort of explosion in the bathroom. It blew part of the wall out. And the handbasin is smashed.'

He didn't seem too bothered, just went over to have a closer look at the damage.

I looked down at my pyjamas again. Every button had been blown exactly in half, leaving just enough thread to hold them on to the fabric.